ANNA'S ART ADVENTURE

Written by

Bjørn Sortland

Illustrated by

Lars Elling

CAROLRHODA BOOKS, INC./MINNEAPOLIS

You are looking forward to this, aren't you?" asked Uncle Harold, who had brought Anna to work with him at the art museum.

Anna nodded.

"Fine," said Uncle Harold. "Now you must be good and keep up while I show some people around. You are not to ask questions or touch anything or get tired and want to sit down or go to the bathroom or ask for candy or soda or run down the halls or want to go home."

"Yes, no, no, no, no, no, no, no," promised Anna.

"This will be fun," said Uncle Harold.

Anna watched the grown-ups who were listening to her uncle.

"Visual art . . . ," Uncle Harold said in a serious voice, "is a vast subject. I shall attempt to explain, so please keep your questions for later."

None of the grown-ups said a thing. They just nodded, coughed, and cleared their throats a bit.

Anna had to go to the bathroom. Now. It didn't matter what her uncle had said. She inched farther and farther away from the others. Because when you've got to go, you've got to go.

"Do you know where the bathroom is?" Anna asked, peering at the laughing face of a wrinkled old man.

"Hmm, ha, ha. There's no point in asking me," said the man. "I, Rembrandt van Rijn, haven't been to the bathroom for more than three hundred years."

"Then why are you laughing?" asked Anna.

"I'm laughing so that I won't look too serious. I'm so much older than the others hanging in here that I'm worried no one will want to look at me. In fact, Marcel Duchamp got so bored with all the old pictures that he exhibited a disgusting little toilet and called it art. I'm sure you'll find it if you look."

Had Duchamp exhibited a real toilet or a piece of art? Anna had to find out because she really had to go.

She spotted a red dress on the floor. Who had left a dress here? Had another girl needed the bathroom in a hurry, too?

Anna looked around, but she didn't see anyone without clothes on. She quickly looked around again and then picked up the mysterious red dress. When she pushed her head through the neck of the dress, she suddenly discovered . . .

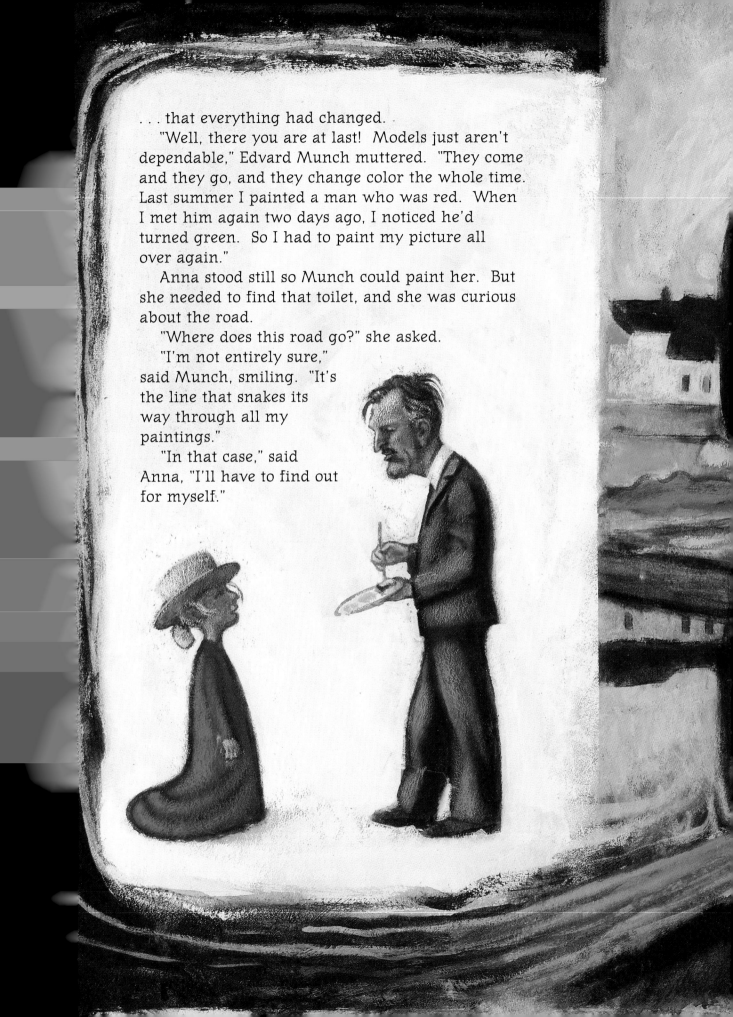

. . . that everything had changed.

"Well, there you are at last! Models just aren't dependable," Edvard Munch muttered. "They come and they go, and they change color the whole time. Last summer I painted a man who was red. When I met him again two days ago, I noticed he'd turned green. So I had to paint my picture all over again."

Anna stood still so Munch could paint her. But she needed to find that toilet, and she was curious about the road.

"Where does this road go?" she asked.

"I'm not entirely sure," said Munch, smiling. "It's the line that snakes its way through all my paintings."

"In that case," said Anna, "I'll have to find out for myself."

As Anna walked down the road,
it became a straight black line that
led into other straight black lines.
She balanced her way along a black
line that divided a white area and a
red area. "The big red area could
be a strawberry field," she thought.
"And that blue area over there
could be a blueberry field."

Anna approached a yellow field
where a man in a yellow straw hat
was painting. Maybe he knew
something about Duchamp's toilet.

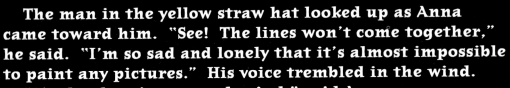

The man in the yellow straw hat looked up as Anna came toward him. "See! The lines won't come together," he said. "I'm so sad and lonely that it's almost impossible to paint any pictures." His voice trembled in the wind.

"Maybe there's too much wind," said Anna.

"No, no. It's me——I'm shaking too much. Now they'll never buy any paintings by Vincent van Gogh! Just think, I've painted all these lovely colors——sulfur yellow, ochre yellow, lemon yellow, the pale yellow of lemonade——but no one wants my pictures." He sighed.

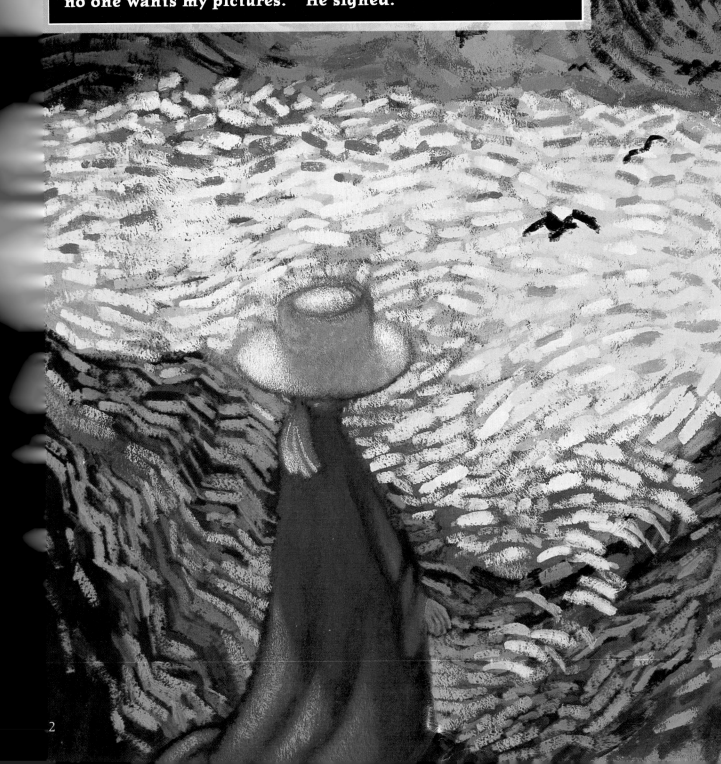

"Just don't think about lemonade," thought Anna, crossing her legs. "Yellow's really cool," she said, and she hurried through the field.

A little man was holding a huge parasol above a woman who hadn't quite decided where her nose should go.

"Dora and I were just about to have a snack," the man said to Anna. "You're in luck. There's enough for you, too."

"And please, call me Pablo," said Pablo Picasso.

Anna smiled when she saw Pablo's snack—square apples and triangular pears. The artist's eyes twinkled slyly.

"Nice, aren't they?" he said. "In my paintings, you can see one thing from several sides. For example, you can sit right here and look at Dora's nose from every angle. I paint in this way so you can really *see* a nose. I'd like to paint your nose, too."

But Anna had no time to do any more modeling. She had to find out about that toilet.

Farther down the beach, a pale man in a dark suit was selling soup. "Want to buy some tomato soup? Chicken soup? Andy's art soup?" he asked. "I painted it myself."

"Are you a soup-seller or a painter?" asked Anna.

"Well, both. I'm soup-artist and super-artist Andy Warhol, and I run an entire art factory."

"But isn't it boring just painting cans of soup?"

"Oh, I can make art out of anything—soup cans, movie stars, Coke bottles, money. It doesn't matter. Most people only want a picture that matches the living room sofa." Andy shrugged his shoulders. "And you can make money selling soup cans."

"You'd make more money selling ice cream here," said Anna with a yawn. She was beginning to feel warm and sleepy. Anna settled herself on the sand and closed her eyes. "If only I could simply fly to that bathroom," she thought.

Elling

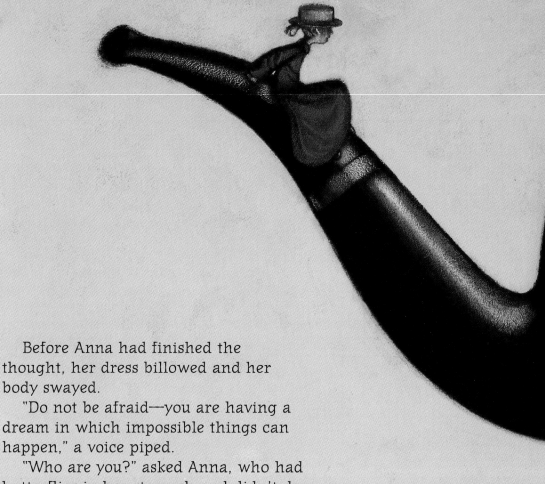

Before Anna had finished the
thought, her dress billowed and her
body swayed.

"Do not be afraid—you are having a
dream in which impossible things can
happen," a voice piped.

"Who are you?" asked Anna, who had
butterflies in her stomach and didn't dare open
her eyes.

"I am a painting. I am Nothing or Anything. I am
Everything You Can Dream Of—a blazing giraffe,
a fish-lion, a piano-egg. *But I am definitely not a pipe,*"
piped the voice.

"And if I dream you're nothing at all?" asked Anna.

"Then I will dis . . . app . . . e . . . a . . . r . . ."

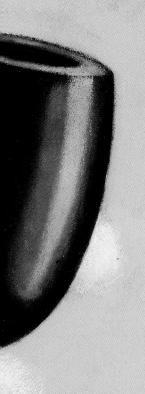

And before Anna could dream of anything,
she was falling,

falling,

falling...

. . . until someone suddenly grabbed her hand, and
Anna found herself dangling in midair.

"Hello, little angel," said Marc Chagall. "What
a fantastic surprise to get a visit from heaven.
Would you mind dangling in the air
just a little longer so that I can paint
you? Hens, horses, and houses all need
a little help to fly. But angels can
manage by themselves."

"Would you please pull me back to earth?"
asked Anna. "I've got to find the . . ."

The painter vanished, and Anna was left holding a round, green apple.

"That's a nice apple you've got there. It's exactly the kind of apple I need," mumbled the man fidgeting by Anna's side. "I've spent the whole day looking for an apple like that. Mine are starting to rot, so I have to get new ones. You haven't taken a bite out of it, have you?"

"No," replied Anna. "I just got it."

The man seemed a little restless. Maybe *he* had to go to the bathroom, too.

"I'll give it to you," Anna said, "if I can *see* what you use it for."

"Come along, then," said the man.

"You've set the table so beautifully," said Anna. "Do you have company coming?"

"No, no," said the man. "I do still lifes—paintings of natural objects on a table. I don't want to paint any more people because I'm too shy. Apples are better. They don't wilt like flowers. They stay quite still and speak to me of rain and sun, scent and color."

Anna placed the apple carefully on the table.

"No, not there," the man said.

Anna moved the apple a tiny bit.

"Hmm, no. That's not quite right, either."

Anna sighed and moved the apple again, a teeny-weeny bit.

"Yes, that's it. Right there." He took out his brush. "Now the world will see what Paul Cézanne can do with an apple!"

Anna was more interested in what Duchamp had done with his toilet. She rushed on to the next room.

"Hey ho. Has old Henri Matisse got a caller?"

Anna stared at the painter. He gave his long bamboo paintbrush a slight twiddle, and suddenly a gaily colored woman appeared!

"Is it easy to make pictures of women like that?" Anna asked. She was beginning to like the idea of doing some painting herself.

"Well, yes." Matisse smiled. "I relax when I paint. Looking at my pictures should be like sitting in a comfortable armchair."

Anna could have stood there all day watching Matisse conjure up women, if she didn't need to find that toilet.

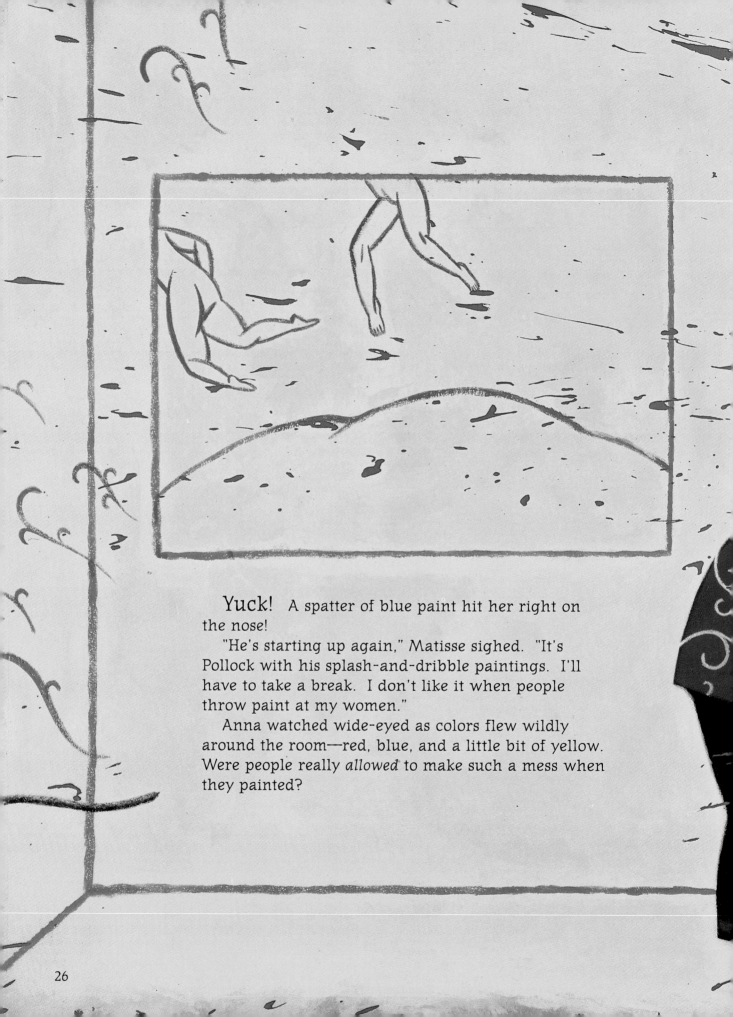

Yuck! A spatter of blue paint hit her right on the nose!

"He's starting up again," Matisse sighed. "It's Pollock with his splash-and-dribble paintings. I'll have to take a break. I don't like it when people throw paint at my women."

Anna watched wide-eyed as colors flew wildly around the room—red, blue, and a little bit of yellow. Were people really *allowed* to make such a mess when they painted?

"Do you have permission to do this?"
Anna asked the man who was painting all
over the floor.

"I never get permission," said Jackson
Pollock. "I make as much of a mess as I
want."

"Lucky you!" said Anna. "I'm not
allowed to do anything here. My uncle
tells me what to do and what not to do.
I bet he'd even like to tell the paintings
what to look like."

"Paintings decide for themselves," the
artist said. "I just dribble a few colors.
Here—you try it."

"Mmm. It smells wonderful," thought Anna as she dipped a brush into a can of beautiful, thick paint.

She began with a small dab of yellow. Then a blue stripe. Suddenly, the colors took over— a splash here and a splash there, a big glob here and a small glob there.

All Anna had to do was move the brush. She had nearly forgotten how desperately she needed to go.

But only nearly.

"Can you tell me where Duchamp's toilet is?" she asked. "You see, I've really, really got to . . ."

"Toilet? Oh, you must mean Duchamp's *Fountain*," said Pollock. "That's been up in my attic for years. But I don't really see how you can . . ."

But when you've got to go, you've got to go.
Anna raced up the stairs and threw open
the door to the attic. Then she stopped dead in
her tracks.

There it was. It didn't look like art, but it
wasn't a toilet, either. Duchamp's *Fountain*
was an old, dusty, useless *urinal*. How was she
supposed to use *that*?

It was a disappointment, to say the least.

"Naturally," thought Anna. "Naturally, it would be a urinal. It's men who've decided what everything should look like in this story. It's a good thing *I* managed to paint one picture!"

Anna looked at the clock. It was getting late. How would she ever find her way back to where she was supposed to be? She looked down at the mysterious red dress that seemed to have caused her whole adventure. Slowly, Anna pulled the dress off over her head and discovered . . .

. . . that she was back with Uncle Harold again.

"The interesting thing," Uncle Harold said in rather a tired voice, "is that here one can see how Pollock, just by mixing a little paint, has created this well-known painting. In principle, one might say that it's simple to create art—just mix red, blue, and a little bit of yellow and follow all the rules of painting."

Uncle Harold took a final, long, artistic pause.

"My child could have painted that," whispered a lady with a long neck.

"Uncle Harold doesn't know everything about art and artists," thought Anna. "He doesn't know who really painted that picture or what can happen if you venture into a painting."

But Anna knew—she had tried it for herself.

In her sweetest voice Anna asked, "Uncle Harold? Can you tell me where the bathroom is?"

Because when you've got to go, you've just got to go.

Here are the painters and pictures Anna saw at the museum:

page 6
Rembrandt van Rijn (1606—1669)
was a Dutch painter who lived a long time before the other artists in this book. He painted landscapes, still lifes, and biblical scenes, but he was most fascinated with the portrayal of a single figure. Using warm colors and a great contrast between light and dark in his portraits, he revealed the depths of a person's being. Rembrandt painted close to a hundred self-portraits. *Self-Portrait* (1665), the picture of Rembrandt that Anna talked to, is in the Wallraf-Richartz Museum in Cologne, Germany. When Rembrandt died, he was poor and forgotten, yet he has come to be considered one of the greatest painters of all time.

pages 8-9
Edvard Munch (1863—1944) was a Norwegian painter and graphic artist who painted because he wanted to help himself, and others, understand life. He expressed his ideas with color and line— "music from the inner pictures of my soul," he said. He painted many portraits, both of himself and others, often showing a person's loneliness and helplessness. Munch's observation of people and nature varied according to the mood he was in. "Art grows out of joy and sorrow—mainly sorrow. It grows out of man's life," he said. He called his pictures "my children" and hated selling them. *The Girls on the Pier* (1901), the picture that Anna joined, is in the Nasjonalgalleriet in Oslo, Norway. Eventually, Munch painted 18 different versions of *The Girls on the Pier*.

pages 10-11
Piet Mondrian (1872—1944) was born in the Netherlands and is best known for his abstract paintings of colored rectangles. He wanted to put regular lines and colors together, and he didn't care if the picture "looked like" something. He was more concerned with showing the order and unity of nature. Although his paintings look simple, they show that he had an amazing sense of balance and harmony, which influenced modern architecture. When he was working on one of his many abstract paintings with their black lines and red, blue, and yellow rectangles, he often used a ruler. You can see his abstract paintings in many museums, including the Minneapolis Institute of Arts, the Dallas Museum of Art, and the Museum of Modern Art in New York City.

pages 12-13
Vincent van Gogh (1853—1890) was also Dutch. He was an art dealer, teacher, and minister before he started painting. "God is in all great art," he wrote in one of his many letters to his brother Theo. For years, Theo gave Vincent enough money to live on so that he could paint. His first pictures were

in heavy, dark colors, but after meeting the Impressionists in Paris, he used strong, bright colors. "How beautiful this yellow is!" he wrote. He loved the yellow of sunflowers. He thought it was more important to bring out the unique quality in his subject than to paint it perfectly. Despite his boundless zest for life, van Gogh was often extremely lonely and depressed. He wrote to Theo: "It's not my fault I can't sell my pictures. But there will come a time when people will realize they are worth more than the value of the paint in them." In 1990, one of his paintings sold for $82.5 million, at the time the highest price ever paid for a painting. *Wheat Field with Crows* (1890) may be the last picture he painted. You can see it in the Rijksmuseum Vincent van Gogh in Amsterdam, Netherlands.

pages 14-15
Pablo Picasso (1881—1973) was Spanish, but he lived and worked in France for most of his life. He did an enormous number of pictures, drawings, prints, and sculptures. As a child, he studied art with his father and mastered great technical skills. After the death of his closest friend, he painted pictures of sad, forlorn people in shades of blue. This was called his Blue Period. He painted circus performers in warmer colors during his Rose Period. Later, he began to show all the sides of his subject in a new style called Cubism. These paintings include the picture of the apples and pears in *Bread and Fruit Dish on a Table* (1908-1909), which is in the Kunstmuseum in Basel, Switzerland, and a picture of the lady that Anna meets on the beach, *Dora Maar Seated* (1937), which is in the Musée Picasso in Paris. "Everyone wants to understand art. But why don't they try to understand birdsong?" Picasso asked. For him, it was more important to enjoy the things we like than to be able to understand them.

page 17
Andy Warhol (1930?—1987) was a bit coy about his birthday, so no one is quite certain when he was born. He played tricks with his appearance, too, dyeing his hair yellow or wearing a wig and huge dark glasses. Warhol wanted to create art from simple, impersonal, everyday objects, for example, Campbell's soup cans. You can see his prints of Campbell's soup cans in the Yale University Art Galley in New Haven, Connecticut, and the Leo Castelli Gallery in New York. Warhol also wanted his art to be anonymous, so his assistants at his New York studio called "The Factory" printed the same picture several times. "Making money is art, working is art—doing good business deals is the greatest art," Warhol said. He often created pictures of rich and famous celebrities and eventually became a celebrity himself.

pages 18-19

René Magritte (1898—1967) was the Belgian artist who painted the pipe that took Anna flying. The picture of the pipe is called *The Treachery of Images (This Is No Pipe)* (1929). You can see it in the County Museum of Art, Los Angeles. Like other Surrealists, Magritte painted everyday objects in a realistic style and placed them in strange and unusual surroundings; for example, he painted a train coming from a fireplace. These ordinary but unrelated images together created striking and stimulating compositions. He called this style Magic Realism.

page 20

Marc Chagall (1887—1985) was a Russian Jew who settled in France and later in New York during World War II. "When Chagall paints, you don't know if he's asleep or awake. There must be an angel somewhere in his head," Picasso said of him. Chagall brought dreamlike colors and floating figures into his pictures, giving them a joyous quality. He believed that the things inside us are more real than what we see with our eyes. Many of his paintings show his homeland, Russia, or the lives and dramatic history of the Israeli people. He also decorated several famous buildings around the world and designed the sets and costumes for Stravinsky's ballet *The Firebird*. Before Anna came into the picture, his beloved wife, Bella, dangled in the air in the painting *The Stroll* (1917), which is in the Russian Museum in St. Petersburg, Russia.

pages 21-23

Paul Cézanne (1839—1906) who liked apples so much, was French. His father was a banker and owned a hat factory, and Paul was given enough money to allow him to spend his life painting. He moved away from Paris in order to be able to paint alone in peace and quiet. Cézanne's pictures took shape through his use of bright colors, and they have a harmony and a special calm about them. In his still lifes, he often made flat surfaces appear tilted, like the table in this picture. His still lifes with apples can be seen in the Museum of Modern Art in New York City, the Dallas Museum of Art, and the Fogg Art Museum at Harvard in Cambridge, Massachusetts. "Art must make us perceive nature as something eternal," he said. Cézanne is said to be the father of modern painting. He influenced many painters, including Picasso and Matisse.

pages 24-27

Henri Matisse (1869—1954) was also French. He said, "I'm trying to create art that will be understood by all who see it." Like Cézanne, he painted clear, peaceful, and harmonious pictures. He wanted to get rid of details and simplify line and color. He used both soft and hard lines as well as bright, vivid colors to show a sense of movement and delight. Anna watched him paint *The Dance* (1909–1910), a picture that demonstrates this clearly. You can see one version of *The Dance* at the Museum of Modern Art in New York City and another in the Hermitage in St. Petersburg, Russia.

pages 28-30
Jackson Pollock (1912—1956) was the American who allowed Anna to paint with him. Pollock painted with sticks, trowels, and knives, as well as a great deal of nervous energy, to create "action paintings." While he was painting, he wanted to feel like part of the picture himself, to "walk around in it, work from the four sides and be literally 'in' the painting," he said. He thought that the interaction between himself, the paint, and the canvas was more important than the final result. So he often dribbled and squirted paint across huge canvases stretched out on the floor. You can see Pollock's splash-and-dribble paintings at the Museum of Modern Art in New York City and the National Gallery of Art in Washington, D.C.

page 32
Marcel Duchamp (1887—1968) was from France. He created works that challenged the definition of art. He exhibited all sorts of things—a bicycle wheel in *Bicycle Wheel* (1913), which is in the Museum of Modern Art in New York City, and the controversial urinal *Fountain* (1917). A copy of *Fountain* is in the Philadelphia Museum of Art. He chose ordinary subjects because he didn't want people to take art too seriously. His belief was that people themselves decide what is valuable in art. One of the results of Duchamp's work is that it gave artists an atmosphere of creative freedom. Duchamp once painted a mustache and beard on a copy of Leonardo da Vinci's famous painting *Mona Lisa*.

page 33
Salvador Dali (1904—1989) was a Spanish artist who painted dreams and imaginative madness into his pictures. The clock that Anna sees in the attic is in the picture *The Persistence of Memory* (1931), which you can see in the Museum of Modern Art in New York City. The idea for the painting came to him when he ate some melted Camembert cheese. "The sharks of time shall devour them like flounder fillets," he said.

page 34
Anna is a seven-year-old girl who painted *The Toilet Hunt* (1999), found only on page 34 of this book. You may notice a suspicious resemblance to a painting by Jackson Pollock.

This edition published in 1999 by Carolrhoda Books, Inc.
Translated by James Anderson

Copyright © 1993 by Det Norske Samlaget
First published in Norway in 1993 by Det Norske Samlaget, Oslo, under
the title RAUDT, BLÅTT OG LITT GULT.

Carolrhoda Books, Inc.
A division of Lerner Publishing Group
241 First Avenue North
Minneapolis, MN 55401 U.S.A.

Website address: www.lernerbooks.com

Library of Congress Cataloging-in-Publication Data

Sortland, Bjørn, 1968–
      [Raudt, blått og litt gult. English.]
      Anna's art adventure / by Bjørn Sortland : illustrated by Lars
Elling.
          p.   cm.
      Summary: On her search for the art museum's bathroom, Anna
meets famous artists, becomes part of some of their paintings, and
makes her own art.
      ISBN 1–57505–376–4 (lib. bdg. : alk. paper)
      [l. Art appreciation—Fiction. 2. Artists—Fiction. 3. Museums—
Fiction.] I. Elling, Lars, ill. II. Title.
PZ7.S7218An 1999   98–49049
[E]–dc21

Manufactured in the United States of America
   5 6 7 8 9 – JR – 08 07 06 05